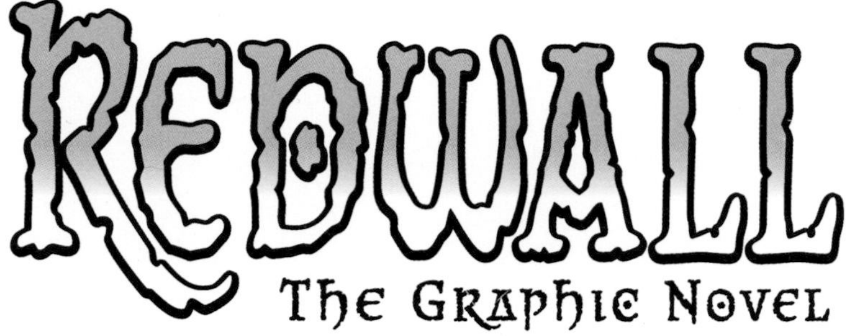
REDWALL
The Graphic Novel

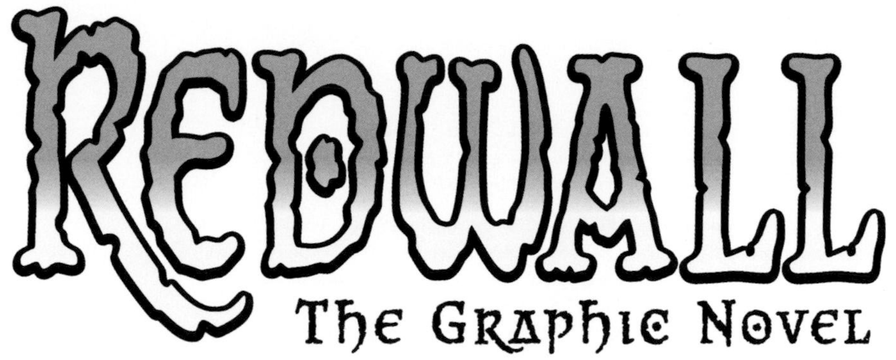

BY BRIAN JACQUES

ILLUSTRATED BY BRET BLEVINS

ADAPTED BY STUART MOORE

LETTERING BY RICHARD STARKINGS

PHILOMEL BOOKS

PHILOMEL BOOKS
A division of Penguin Young Readers Group.
Published by The Penguin Group.

Penguin Group (USA) Inc., 375 Hudson Street, New York, NY 10014, U.S.A.
Penguin Group (Canada), 90 Eglinton Avenue East, Suite 700, Toronto, Ontario, Canada M4P 2Y3
(a division of Pearson Penguin Canada Inc.).
Penguin Books Ltd, 80 Strand, London WC2R 0RL, England.
Penguin Ireland, 25 St. Stephen's Green, Dublin 2, Ireland (a division of Penguin Books Ltd.).
Penguin Group (Australia), 250 Camberwell Road, Camberwell, Victoria 3124, Australia
(a division of Pearson Australia Group Pty Ltd).
Penguin Books India Pvt Ltd, 11 Community Centre, Panchsheel Park, New Delhi - 110 017, India.
Penguin Group (NZ), 67 Apollo Drive, Mairangi Bay, Auckland 1311, New Zealand
(a division of Pearson New Zealand Ltd.)
Penguin Books (South Africa) (Pty) Ltd, 24 Sturdee Avenue, Rosebank, Johannesburg 2196, South Africa.
Penguin Books Ltd, Registered Offices: 80 Strand, London WC2R 0RL, England.

Manufactured in China by South China Printing Co. Ltd.

Library of Congress Cataloging-in-Publication Data
Jacques, Brian. Redwall. Summary: When the peaceful life in and around ancient Redwall Abbey is shattered by the arrival of the evil rat Cluny and his villainous hordes, Matthias, a young mouse, determines to find the legendary sword of Martin the Warrior which, he is convinced, will help Redwall's inhabitants destroy the enemy.
[1. Mice—Fiction. 2. Animal—Fiction. 3. Fantasy.] I. Howell, Troy, ill. II. Title.
PZ7.J15317Re 1987 [Fic] 86-25467

ISBN 978-0-399-24481-0
9 10 8

IT WAS THE START OF THE SUMMER OF THE LATE ROSE.

BOOK ONE: THE WALL

MOSSFLOWER COUNTRY SHIMMERED GENTLY IN A PEACEFUL HAZE.

THE ONSET OF AUTUMN WOULD TURN THE LEAVES INTO A CAPE OF FIERY HUE, THUS ADDING FURTHER GLORY TO THE NAME AND LEGEND...

WHOOPS!

OUCH!
BUMP

FATHER ABBOT!
SORRY -- I JUST -- I TRIPPED ON MY ABBOT, FATHER HABIT.
OH DEAR -- I MEAN --

OH, MATTHIAS... MY SON...
WHEN WILL YOU LEARN TO TAKE LIFE A LITTLE SLOWER?
TO WALK WITH DIGNITY AND HUMILITY?

COME, MATTHIAS.
IT IS TIME WE TALKED TOGETHER.

WHAT IS IT, MY SON?
WHAT ARE YOU LOOKING AT?
OH...FATHER ABBOT...
IF ONLY I COULD BE LIKE *MARTIN THE WARRIOR!*

WE ARE MICE OF PEACE.

OH, I KNOW MARTIN WAS A WARRIOR MOUSE -- BUT THOSE WERE WILD DAYS WHEN STRENGTH WAS NEEDED.

THE STRENGTH OF A CHAMPION.

"HE ARRIVED HERE IN THE DEEP WINTER, WHEN THE FOUNDERS WERE UNDER ATTACK FROM MANY FOXES, VERMIN, AND A GREAT WILDCAT.

"SO FIERCE A FIGHTER WAS MARTIN THAT HE FACED THE ENEMY SINGLE-PAWED, DRIVING THEM MERCILESSLY, FAR FROM MOSSFLOWER.

"HE EMERGED VICTORIOUS AFTER SLAYING THE WILDCAT WITH HIS ANCIENT SWORD, WHICH BECAME FAMOUS THROUGHOUT THE LAND.
"BUT IN THE LAST BLOODY COMBAT MARTIN WAS SERIOUSLY WOUNDED. HE LAY INJURED IN THE SNOW UNTIL THE MICE FOUND HIM."

AS MARTIN RECOVERED, HE WAS TRANSFORMED. HE BEGAN TO LONG FOR PEACE.
HE FORSOOK THE WAY OF THE WARRIOR -- AND HUNG UP HIS SWORD.

THAT WAS WHEN OUR ORDER FOUND ITS TRUE VOCATION.
ALL THE MICE TOOK A SOLEMN VOW NEVER TO HARM ANOTHER LIVING CREATURE --
--UNLESS IT WAS AN ENEMY THAT SOUGHT TO HARM US BY VIOLENCE.

POOR MATTHIAS. ALAS FOR YOUR AMBITIONS.
THE DAY OF THE WARRIOR IS GONE, MY SON. YOU NEED ONLY THINK OF OBEYING ME, YOUR ABBOT, AND DOING AS YOU ARE BIDDEN.
IN TIME TO COME -- WHEN I AM LONG GONE TO MY REST -- YOU WILL THINK BACK TO THIS DAY --
-- AND BLESS MY MEMORY.

COME NOW, MY YOUNG FRIEND -- CHEER UP. IT IS THE SUMMER OF THE LATE ROSE.
TONIGHT WE HAVE A GREAT FEAST TO CELEBRATE -- MY GOLDEN JUBILEE AS ABBOT.

AND AFTERWARD -- I HAVE A SPECIAL ERRAND FOR YOU.
THE CHURCHMOUSE FAMILY HAVE A LONG WAY HOME ON FOOT, AND THERE ARE SO MANY OF THEM. PERHAPS YOU COULD DRIVE THEM HOME TONIGHT, IN THE ABBEY CART.

YOU WILL BE THEIR BODYGUARD, MATTHIAS.
TAKE A GOOD STOUT STAFF WITH YOU.

LEAVE IT TO ME, FATHER ABBOT.
I'LL TAKE FULL RESPONSIBILITY!

OH DEAR.
I'LL HAVE TO GET THAT YOUNG MOUSE SOME SANDALS THAT AREN'T SO BIG...!

HE WAS A GOD OF WAR.

HE WAS A TOUGH, EVIL, FOUL BILGE RAT.
HE WAS THE BIGGEST, MOST SAVAGE RODENT THAT EVER JUMPED FROM SHIP TO SHORE.
CLUNY WAS COMING!
HIS EYE HAD BEEN TORN OUT IN BATTLE WITH A PIKE.
CLUNY HAD LOST AN EYE...
...THE PIKE HAD LOST ITS LIFE.
SKULLFACE!

BUT CHIEF --

IT MIGHT BITE ME BACK!

KRAKKKK

MUTINY! INSUBORDINATION!
BY THE TEETH OF HELL, I'LL FLAY YOU INTO MANGY DOLLRAGS!
NO! NO MORE! DON'T WHIP ME, CHIEF!

LOOK --
-- I'M DOING IT --

NEEEEEEEEE!
AAAHHHH!

NEEEEEEEEE!
HELP!
CLOPACLOPACLOPACLOPA

CLOPA CLOPA CLOPA CLOPA
AAAHHHH!

THANK YOU, SKULLFACE....
CLOPA CLOPA CLOPA CLOPA

CLOPA CLOPA CLOPA CLOPA
TELL THE DEVIL CLUNY SENT YOU!

TELL HIM I'VE COME TO MOSSFLOWER --
-- AND ITS PRECIOUS ABBEY --
-- TO DO HIS WORK.
REDWALL ABBEY 15 MILES
CLOPA CLOPA CLOPA CLOPA

DOWN THE ROAD...
AREN'T THEY SWEET?
THEY'RE FAST ASLEEP!

I'M NOT SURPRISED. THAT WAS QUITE A FEAST!
YES, IT WAS.
IT'S VERY KIND OF YOU TO TAKE ME HOME, MATTHIAS.

IT'S NO TROUBLE, CORNFLOWER. YOU LIVE SO CLOSE TO THE CHURCH...IT'S ONLY SENSIBLE.
BUT IT'S VERY KIND OF *YOU* TO SIT NEXT TO ME!

CLOPACLOPA
CLOPACLOPA
UH-OH...

CONSTANCE?
WHAT IS IT? WHERE ARE YOU GOING?
CLOPA
CLOPA
CLOPA
CLOPA

CONSTANCE!
HANG ON!

CLOPACLOPACLOPA
WHAT'S --
QUIET!

CLOPACLOPA
CLOPACLOPA
LOOK!

DID... DID YOU SEE *THAT?*

I SAW IT, BUT I DON'T BELIEVE IT!

CLOPA
CLOPA
CLOPA
CLOPA

CLOPA
CLOPA

I THINK WE'D BEST HEAD BACK FOR THE ABBEY.
FATHER ABBOT'LL WANT TO KNOW ABOUT THIS STRAIGHTAWAY.
RIGHT.

WE'D BEST RETURN ACROSS THE NORTH MEADOW AND AVOID THE ROAD.
CORNFLOWER, PLEASE TAKE CHARGE OF THE MOTHERS AND BABIES.

MATTHIAS?

DON'T WORRY.
I'LL KEEP WATCH.

SOON...

PAY ATTENTION, EVERYONE!

CONSTANCE AND MATTHIAS...WOULD YOU PLEASE TELL THE COUNCIL OF ELDERS WHAT YOU SAW TONIGHT ON THE ROAD TO ST. NINIAN'S?

RATS, FATHER ABBOT. ***HUNDREDS*** OF THEM.

HEADED THIS WAY IN A RUNAWAY CART.

EVIL RATS! NONSENSE!
PURE SPECULATION!
MATTHIAS... DID YOU NOTICE ANYTHING SPECIAL ABOUT THIS LEADER-RAT?

HE WAS MUCH BIGGER THAN THE OTHERS, FATHER.
HE HAD ONLY ONE EYE --
-- AND HIS *TAIL*...

IT MUST HAVE BEEN THE LONGEST TAIL OF ANY RAT ALIVE.
HE HELD IT IN HIS CLAW AS IF IT WERE A WHIP.

TWICE IN MY LIFETIME I HAVE HEARD TRAVELERS SPEAK OF THIS RAT. HE BEARS A NAME THAT A FOX WOULD BE AFRAID TO WHISPER IN THE DARKNESS OF MIDNIGHT.

CLUNY THE SCOURGE!

CLUNY? WHY, HE'S JUST A FOLK LEGEND!
"GO TO SLEEP OR CLUNY WILL GET YOU!"
HE IS QUITE REAL. BUT I SEE YOU NEED CONVINCING.

I THINK WE REQUIRE THE SERVICES OF --

" -- BROTHER METHUSELAH."

HMMM, HMMM, ME LORD ABBOT CEDRIC...AH, NO, IT'S MORTIMER, ISN'T IT? YOU CAME AFTER CEDRIC...

I SEE SO MANY OF THEM COME AND GO, YOU KNOW.

AH YES...HERE IT IS...

Cluny the Scourge

I REFER TO A RECORD OF WINTER, SIX YEARS BACK...

IT SEEMS THAT THIS RAT -- CLUNY, THEY CALLED HIM --

-- WANTED TO SETTLE HIS ARMY IN A MINE OWNED BY BADGERS.

WHEN THE BADGERS DROVE HIM OUT, CLUNY RETURNED BY NIGHT...AND WITH HIS BAND OF RATS GNAWED AWAY AT THE WOODEN SHORING, CAUSING THE MINE TO COLLAPSE THE NEXT DAY -- KILLING THE OWNERS.

I CAN RECITE OTHER MISDEEDS FROM MEMORY. THE HORDES OF CLUNY THE SCOURGE HAVE MOVED SOUTHWARD OVER THE PAST SIX YEARS.

A FARMHOUSE SET ALIGHT...AN ENTIRE LITTER OF PIGLETS EATEN ALIVE BY RATS...A HERD OF COWS STAMPEDED THROUGH A VILLAGE, CAUSING CHAOS AND MUCH DESTRUCTION.

WHY, THANK YOU, MATTHIAS.

I COULD NOT HAVE PUT IT BETTER MYSELF.

"WE'LL BE READY."

DIE...
DIE...

AARRRHHH!

NO...
NO!!
CHIEF?
UUHH!
UH... CHIEF?
YOU ALL RIGHT?
WE'VE GOT THE NEW RECRUITS TOGETHER. MORE THAN A HUNDRED RATS, FERRETS, AND WEASELS.
WE'RE READY.
THEN READ 'EM THE ARTICLES...
AND LET'S GO...

THEY'RE RINGING THAT BELL AGAIN, CHIEF. MAYBE THEY THINK IT'LL FRIGHTEN US OFF!

SHUT YOUR MOUTH, FOOL.

REDTOOTH?

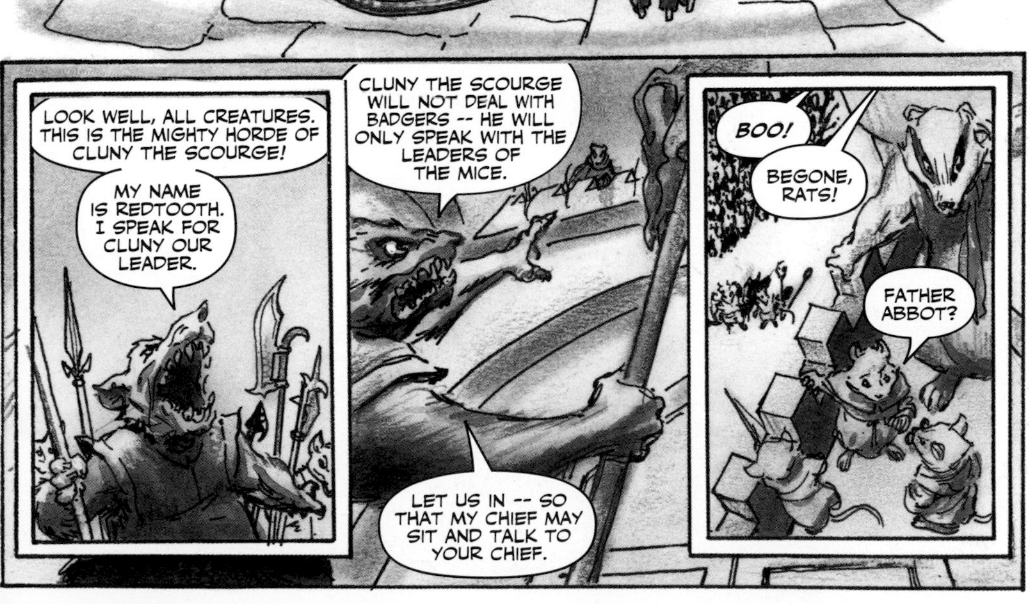

YOU THERE, AND YOU ALSO. MY ABBOT WILL TALK WITH YOU BOTH.
THE REST MUST REMAIN OUTSIDE.

NEVER!
EAT THE MICE!
WE AGREE, MOUSE.
LET US IN!

PUT DOWN YOUR WEAPONS, RATS. THROW OFF YOUR ARMOR TO SHOW US THAT YOU COME IN PEACE.
YOU -- CLUNY THE SCOURGE -- WE KNOW OF YOUR TAIL. IT, TOO, IS A WEAPON.
KNOT IT TIGHTLY AROUND YOUR WAIST SO THAT IT CANNOT BE USED.
HA HA HA!
YOUNG MOUSE -- YOU DO RIGHT TO ASK THIS THING --
-- FOR TRULY YOU ARE LOOKING AT CLUNY THE SCOURGE.
KRAKKKKK

AND SO...

SATAN'S NOSE, CHIEF! THERE'S A PRETTY ONE FOR YOU!
PLEASE. SIT.

NOW... MY SON...
WHAT DO YOU WANT AT REDWALL ABBEY?

HA HA HA HA HA!
YOUR SON! THAT'S A GOOD ONE!

I'LL TELL YOU WHAT I WANT, MOUSE. I WANT IT *ALL.*
THE LOT. EVERYTHING.
DO YOU HEAR ME?!

READ THEM THE ARTICLES.

WHY PICK ON A SMALL MOUSE?

SURELY A BIG STRONG RAT LIKE YOU CAN DEAL WITH AN OLD BADGER!

COME ON -- TRY *ME* FOR SIZE!

YOU -- ABBOT MOUSE --
YOU HAVE UNTIL TOMORROW EVENING TO GIVE ME YOUR ANSWER.
I WILL NOT NEED UNTIL TOMORROW, RAT.

I TELL YOU RIGHT NOW THAT NEITHER YOU NOR YOUR ARMY WILL EVER SET PAW OR CLAW INSIDE REDWALL, NOT WHILE I OR ANY OF MY CREATURES HAVE BREATH IN OUR BODIES TO FIGHT AND RESIST YOU.
THAT IS MY SOLEMN WORD.

THEN *DIE*, ALL OF YOU: EVERY MALE, FEMALE, AND YOUNG ONE.
YOU WILL BEG ON YOUR KNEES FOR DEATH TO COME SWIFTLY -- BUT I SHALL MAKE YOUR TORMENT LOUD AND LONG BEFORE YOU DIE!

CRASH
GET OUT, RATS! LEAVE THIS ABBEY BEFORE I BREAK THE LAWS OF HOSPITALITY FIRST --
-- AND ASK THE ABBOT'S PARDON LATER!

GO, WHILE YOU STILL HAVE SKULLS!
BIG COUNTRY BUMPKIN, EH, CHIEF?
ONE MORE WORD BACK THERE AND SHE'D HAVE THROWN THAT TABLE AT US --
CHIEF?
THAT...
THAT'S THE MOUSE FROM MY DREAMS...
THAT IS *MARTIN THE WARRIOR.*
HE FOUNDED OUR ORDER.
AND I'LL TELL YOU SOMETHING ELSE, RAT.

MARTIN WAS THE BRAVEST MOUSE THAT EVER LIVED.
IF HE WERE HERE TODAY, HE'D TAKE UP HIS BIG SWORD AND SEND YOU AND ALL YOUR BULLIES PACKING --
-- THOSE OF YOU HE DIDN'T CHOP UP INTO CROW MEAT!

NOW GO!

DON'T FORGET TO CALL AGAIN, RAT. I'D BE DELIGHTED TO SEE YOU!
WE'VE GOT SOME UNFINISHED BUSINESS!

FORM UP, EVERYONE!
BACK TO THE CHURCH!
REDTOOTH...

...GET ME *SHADOW.*
I HAVE A JOB FOR HIM.

"NO BEAST I KNOW OF COULD CLIMB THOSE WALLS, CLUNY."

"EXCEPT YOU?"

"EXCEPT ME."

" -- LEANING ON A SWORD.

"I MUST HAVE THAT PICTURE, SHADOW.

?

"CUT IT, RIP IT, OR TEAR IT OUT. BUT DO NOT FAIL ME --

" -- OR YOUR SCREAMS WILL BE HEARD FAR BEYOND THE WOODLAND AND MEADOWS!"

MATTHIAS...
UUHHHH...?
MATTHIAS, I NEED YOU. HELP...
YOU MUST HELP ME QUICKLY!

UNNFF!
PLOP

A... A RAT?

BOOMP

STOP HIM!

STOP THAT RAT!

STOP --

UUH!

AAAAHHH!

UUUHHH...
SURRENDER, RAT.
I'VE GOT YOU --

AAHHH!

WAPPPP

CRUNCH

CLUNY...
I'M HURT...

HELP ME...

SWIP

GET UP AND RUN FOR IT OR STAY THERE, FOOL.
I DON'T CARRY CRIPPLES AND BUNGLERS!

THERE HE IS!
BUT...THE TAPESTRY...

IT'S GOT TO BE HERE SOMEWHERE...

TOO LATE... MOUSE...
TAPESTRY IS WITH... CLUNY NOW.

*

DAWN.

CHIEF --

THE HORDE IS READY TO MARCH!

BEHOLD MY **NEW** BATTLE FLAG!

THAT IS MARTIN THE WARRIOR --

-- SUPPOSED PROTECTOR OF THAT DODDERING OLD ABBOT AND HIS WITLESS MOB OF MICE.

BUT NOW THAT MARTIN IS MINE -- HE WILL LEAD US TO VICTORY!

SLEEPING AT YOUR POSTS! ALLOWING THE ENEMY INTO OUR ABBEY TO STEAL THAT WHICH WE HOLD MOST DEAR!
IS THIS THE WAY YOU DEFEND US?

IS THIS -- ?

FORGIVE ME, MY FRIENDS. I CRITICIZE YOU UNJUSTLY.
WE ARE ALL CREATURES OF PEACE -- UNSKILLED IN THE ART OF WAR. AND MARTIN THE WARRIOR IS GONE FROM THE ABBEY.
WITHOUT HIM AMONG US --

" -- WE ARE FORSAKEN."
HMMM...
THIS COULD PRESENT A LITTLE PROBLEM...

A LITTLE PROBLEM?
WELL, AT LEAST IT'S NOT A FULLY-GROWN ADULT PROBLEM!
* SQUEAK! *

BASIL STAG HARE AT YOUR SERVICE, SIR!
EXPERT SCOUT, HINDLEG FIGHTER, WILDERNESS GUIDE, AND LIBERATOR OF TENDER YOUNG CROPS, CARROTS, LETTUCE, AND OTHER SUCH STRANGE BEASTS.
PRAY TELL ME WHO I HAVE THE PLEASURE OF ADDRESSING, AND PLEASE STATE THE NATURE OF YOUR LITTLE PROBLEM!

UH --
GOOD DAY TO YOU, MR. BASIL STAG HARE. MY NAME IS MATTHIAS -- I AM A NOVICE IN THE ORDER OF REDWALL MICE.

MY IMMEDIATE PROBLEM IS TO CROSS THIS LAND TO THE CHURCH OVER YONDER WITHOUT BEING DISCOVERED BY THOSE RATS.
HMM, RATS. I KNEW THEY'D COME EVENTUALLY -- COULD FEEL IT IN THE OLD EARS.
AS FOR REDWALL, I KNOW IT WELL. EXCELLENT TYPE, ABBOT MORTIMER. I EVEN HEARD THE JOSEPH BELL TOLLING OUT THE SANCTUARY MESSAGE!

BASIL -- I FEEL RELUCTANT TO ASK YOU TO INVOLVE YOURSELF IN MY FIGHT. BUT --
WOULD IT BE POSSIBLE FOR YOU TO CREATE SOME KIND OF DIVERSION? TO KEEP THE RATS BUSY WHILE I'M GETTING TO THE CHURCH?
SAY NO MORE, LADDIE.

NEVER LET IT BE SAID THAT BASIL STAG HARE WAS BACKWARD IN COMING FORWARD!

I SAY, OLD THING! WHERE'S THIS LEADER FELLER? CLUNY, OR LOONY, WHATEVER YOU CALL HIM?
PHEW! DON'T YOU CHAPS EVER TAKE A BATH?

A BIG SKINNY RABBIT! GRAB HIM, LADS!
BIG SKINNY RABBIT YOURSELF! CATSMEAT!
I'LL STICK HIS DAMNED GUTS ON MY PIKE!

BLAST! HE'S AS SLIPPERY AS A GREASED PIG!
SOME OF MY BEST FRIENDS ARE GREASED PIGS, BOTTLE NOSE!
OOPS! MISSED ME AGAIN, YOU OLD BUTTERFINGERS!
...
IT'S NOT HERE.
AND NEITHER IS CLUNY'S ARMY.
THEY'VE GONE --

-- TO ATTACK *REDWALL.*

REDTOOTH! DARKCLAW! TELL THE SLING-THROWERS TO STAND READY!

WHEN I GIVE THE SIGNAL, I WANT TO SEE A GOOD HEAVY BARRAGE OF STONES HITTING THE TOP OF THAT PARAPET!

HEAR THAT SCRAPING, CONSTANCE? CLUNY'S LOT ARE PUTTING SOMETHING AGAINST THE WALLS.
THEY'RE TRYING TO CLIMB UP WHILE WE'VE GOT TO LIE LOW!
OH, THEY ARE, ARE THEY?
AAAHH!!

I HAVE A NEW PLAN.
YOU -- SQUAD LEADERS -- SPLIT UP AND SEARCH THE AREA FOR ANY BIG, HIGH TREES GROWING NEAR THE ABBEY WALLS.
THE MICE WON'T SUSPECT A THING. BEFORE THEY CAN GATHER THEIR WITS ABOUT THEM WE'LL BE INSIDE REDWALL.

WHERE'S RAGEAR?
I DON'T KNOW, CHIEF --

" -- HE NEVER CAME BACK FROM PATROL LAST NIGHT."
ASMODEUS...

ASMODEUSSSSSSSSSSSS!

AND INSIDE GREAT HALL...
THE BATTLE RAGES.
METHUSELAH IS TOO OLD FOR ACTIVE SERVICE...

BUT PERHAPS MY FERTILE BRAIN MAY STILL SERVE THE ORDER.
IF ONLY I COULD FIND A CLUE TO THE RESTING PLACE OF MARTIN THE WARRIOR...OR OF HIS ANCIENT SWORD...

I HAVE SEARCHED FOR THEM OVER THE YEARS...BUT, ALAS, WITH NO SUCCESS.
A PITY THAT MATTHIAS CANNOT BE FOUND. WHAT I NEED IS A YOUNGER, FRESHER MIND TO ASSIST ME.
LONG YEARS HAVE TAKEN THEIR TOLL ON --

AH!

END BOOK ONE

BOOK TWO: THE QUEST

WHILE THE RATS CONTINUED THEIR SIEGE OF REDWALL ABBEY...

...NIGHT CLOSED IN ON MATTHIAS, A SMALL MOUSE WANDERING, LOST, IN THE DEPTHS OF MOSSFLOWER WOOD.

HE BEGAN TO DESPAIR OF EVER SEEING REDWALL AGAIN. AND HE BECAME CRITICAL OF HIMSELF: THE GREAT WARRIOR...

...FRIGHTENED OF THE DARK LIKE A BABY CHURCHMOUSE.

SUCK SUCK

* SQUEAK! *

STEADY NOW, CHEESETHIEF --
-- YOU MORON!
MEANWHILE...
ON THE NORTH SIDE OF THE ABBEY...
FAR FROM THE GATEHOUSE WALL...
AND TRY NOT TO MAKE ENOUGH NOISE TO WAKEN THE ENTIRE ABBEY!
CLINK CLUNK
CLUNK
I'LL GO FIRST.
SCRAGG, YOU COME NEXT. THE REST OF YOU FOLLOW.

NO

AAHHHH!
SWACK

AAGGHH!
OOOHH!

BUNK
CLUNK

HOW MANY DID WE GET?
HARD TO TELL IN THIS LIGHT. BUT I'D SWEAR THAT WAS CLUNY THAT CONSTANCE TIPPED OFF THE PLANK.
MAYBE WE'D BETTER GO AND SEE!
MAYBE NOT. THIS COULD BE A DIVERSIONARY TACTIC.

IF IT WAS CLUNY WHO FELL FROM THE PLANK, ALL WELL AND GOOD. BUT IF IT WASN'T, THEN HE'S STILL AROUND THE FRONT, BY THE GATEHOUSE WALL --

" -- AND IT WON'T SERVE ANY USEFUL PURPOSE COUNTING DEAD BODIES."
CHIEF...?

CHIEF!

TRY NOT TO MOVE, CHIEF. LIE STILL.
WE'LL GET YOU BACK TO CAMP.
UHHH....
FOXES...

FIND SELA THE FOX... BRING HER TO ME.
THOSE ABBEY MICE ARE GOING TO PAY WITH BLOOD... FOR WHAT THEY HAVE DONE...

...TO CLUNY THE SCOURGE.

AT DAWN... JUST AS A WEARY MATTHIAS WAS BEGINNING TO DOUBT THAT HIS COMPANION KNEW THE WAY...
SUCK SUCK
PUFF PUFF
OH --
OH MY.
THERE'S NO PLACE LIKE HOME!

WHAT A SPLENDID PATHFINDER YOU ARE, MY FRIEND!
MATTHIAS!
SUCK SUCK

CONSTANCE!

YOU CAN TELL US EVERYTHING LATER, MATTHIAS. RIGHT NOW, I INSIST THAT YOU COME TO THE MAIN GATE.

THERE'S SOMETHING YOU MUST SEE.

SHORTLY, ON THE RAMPARTS...

DISCHARGE NO MISSILES OR WEAPONRY AT THE ENEMY AS THEY RETREAT.

WE MUST TEMPER TRIUMPH WITH MERCY.

BEFORE I FORGET, MATTHIAS -- BROTHER METHUSELAH WOULD LIKE VERY MUCH TO TALK WITH YOU.

"HE IS IN GREAT HALL."

AH, MATTHIAS. THERE YOU ARE.
LOOK HERE. QUITE BY ACCIDENT, I DISCOVERED THIS WRITING BENEATH WHERE MARTIN'S PICTURE ONCE HUNG.

WHAT DOES IT SAY, BROTHER METHUSELAH?
IT'S WRITTEN IN THE OLD HAND... BUT I CAN READ IT CLEARLY ENOUGH.

"WHO SAYS THAT I AM DEAD KNOWS NOUGHT AT ALL. I — AM THAT IS, TWO MICE WITHIN REDWALL. THE WARRIOR SLEEPS 'TWIXT HALL AND CAVERN HOLE. I — AM THAT IS, TAKE ON MY MIGHTY ROLE.
"LOOK FOR THE SWORD IN MOONLIGHT STREAMING FORTH, AT NIGHT, WHEN DAY'S FIRST HOUR REFLECTS THE NORTH. FROM O'ER THE THRESHOLD SEEK AND YOU WILL SEE; I — AM THAT IS, MY SWORD WILL WIELD FOR ME."

WE MUST STUDY THIS BIT BY BIT.
"WHO SAYS THAT I AM DEAD KNOWS NOUGHT AT ALL"...
BUT WE KNOW THAT MARTIN IS DEAD!

LOOK -- "I — AM THAT IS," DO YOU SEE?
THERE IS A SORT OF DASH BETWEEN THE WORDS "I" AND "AM." WHAT DO YOU MAKE OF THAT?
PERHAPS...

"I — AM THAT IS." THAT'S IT!
WHAT? I'M AFRAID I DON'T FOLLOW YOU...
LOOK AT JUST THE LAST THREE WORDS. THEN MIX UP THE LETTERS AND REARRANGE THEM...

"AM THAT IS." MATTHIAS.
IT'S YOUR OWN NAME.

METHUSELAH, DO YOU REALIZE WHAT THIS MEANS?
OH YES. INDEED I DO.
IT MEANS THAT MARTIN SOMEHOW KNEW THAT ONE DAY HE WOULD LIVE ON -- THROUGH YOU!

LOOK AT THESE LINES:
"THE WARRIOR SLEEPS 'TWIXT HALL AND CAVERN HOLE. I — AM THAT IS, TAKE ON MY MIGHTY ROLE."
THAT'S PRETTY CLEAR.
IT MEANS THAT MARTIN, CARRYING ON THROUGH YOU, HAS A GREAT TASK TO PERFORM.

WHAT ABOUT THIS LINE?
"'TWIXT HALL AND CAVERN HOLE"...
-- THERE IS A FLIGHT OF STAIRS!
COME ON!

...FOREMOLE SAYS THE FOURTH STEP IS A TYPE THAT CAN BE TURNED OVER.
YURR MOLES...
GATHER ROUND AN' SET YOUR IGGEN CLAWS N UM CRACK...

CREEEEEEK

MATTHIAS... I FEEL MYSELF IN THE PRESENCE OF ONE MANY TIMES OLDER THAN ME.
COME ON, OLD FRIEND. LET US ENTER TOGETHER...
...THE TOMB OF MARTIN THE WARRIOR.

"O WARRIOR MOUSE --

"PROTECT REDWALL."

SHE MAY BE A FOX, BUT SHE'LL NEVER OUTFOX ME!

OH, *SELA*...

YOUR HEALING POTIONS HAVE MADE ME SLEEPY.

LEAVE ME NOW. I MUST REST.

YES SIR.

CHICKENHOUND!

LISTEN CAREFULLY, MY SON. AND DON'T VEER FROM WHAT I TELL YOU.
I WANT YOU TO RUN AS QUICKLY AS YOU CAN TO REDWALL ABBEY AND DELIVER THIS NOTE.

DO NOT BREATHE A WORD OF THIS TO ANYONE ELSE. BE ON YOUR GUARD.
AND DO NOT LET ME DOWN.
TO THE ABBOT OF REDWALL ABBEY
I KNOW EXACTLY WHEN, WHERE, AND HOW THE HORDES OF CLUNY WILL ATTACK YOUR ABBEY. WHAT PRICE WILL YOU GIVE ME FOR THIS IMPORTANT INFORMATION?
SELA THE VIXEN

I UNDERSTAND, MOTHER.

AH, CLUNY... SOMEDAY, YOU MUST LEARN TO PLAY CHESS.
YOU WOULD BE UNBEATABLE.

SELA HAS TAKEN THE BAIT.
NO DOUBT THE MICE WILL BE INTERESTED TO LEARN OF MY SCHEME TO ATTACK THEIR MAIN GATE -- WITH A BATTERING RAM.

THEY WILL STRENGTHEN THE GATEHOUSE AND DEPLOY THEIR DEFENDERS IN THAT IMMEDIATE AREA.
MEANWHILE...

I WILL BE TUNNELING UNDER THE SOUTHWESTERN CORNER OF THE ABBEY WALL!
HA HA HA HA HA!
NOW....
I CAN CATCH A FEW HOURS' SLEEP...

ATOP REDWALL'S GATEHOUSE...
WELL, WE'RE ABOVE THE THRESHOLD.
THIS OLD ENGRAVING MUST BE WHAT WE'RE LOOKING FOR!
YES. FUNNY HOW I'VE NEVER PAID ATTENTION TO IT BEFORE.
HELLO THERE, YOU TWO!

I JUST MADE AN INTERESTING DEAL WITH A FOX. WE MAY SOON KNOW MUCH MORE OF CLUNY'S NEW PLANS TO ATTACK REDWALL.
WHAT ARE YOU DOING?

TOMORROW NIGHT IS THE FULL MOON, MY DEAR CONSTANCE.
IF WE STAND UP HERE AT ONE O'CLOCK IN THE MORNING, WE MAY BE ABLE TO FIND THE SWORD OF MARTIN THE WARRIOR.
HOW ARE YOU GOING TO MANAGE THAT?

WE'RE NOT QUITE SURE YET.
IT'S ALL LINKED CLOSELY WITH THE RHYME FROM THE WALL OF GREAT HALL, MARTIN'S TOMB, AND THE STUFF WE FOUND IN IT --
-- THIS SWORD BELT, A SHIELD, ANOTHER RHYME ON THE BACK OF A D--
WAIT A MOMENT.
WHAT TYPE OF SHIELD?

OH... PRETTY MUCH THE STANDARD KIND USED BY WARRIORS.
A ROUND STEEL AFFAIR WITH HAND- AND ARM-HOLDS.
YES, I'VE SEEN THAT SORT OF THING BEFORE. NOT MUCH TO LOOK AT...
IN FACT -- JUST THE TYPE OF SHIELD THAT WOULD FIT *PRECISELY* INTO THIS CIRCLE.

LOOK!
THE SHIELD IS REFLECTING THE MOONLIGHT BACK INTO THE SKY!
WAIT. LOOK AT THE ABBEY ROOF.
THE BEAM CUTS RIGHT ACROSS THE TOP GABLE.
I CAN SEE THE WEATHER VANE AS CLEARLY AS IF IT WERE DAY.

"...A SQUIRREL."
CAN SHE DO THIS?
NOT EVEN IN THE OLDEST RECORDED WRITINGS IS THERE ANY MENTION OF A CREATURE CLIMBING SO HIGH...
DON'T WORRY. SHE'S JUST LIMBERING UP.

LOVELY DAY FOR A CLIMB!

ARE YOU ALL RIGHT THERE, JESS?
WELL, I'M MAKING HEADWAY, M'DEAR.
THIS STONE, THOUGH -- IT'S A BIT ROUGH ON THE OLD PAWS AND CLAWS. NOT LIKE GOOD OLD WOOD OR TREE BARK.

WHERE IS SHE NOW? WILL SOMEONE PLEASE ENLIGHTEN ME?
SHE'S ON TOP OF THE ROOF... WALKING TOWARD THE GABLE...

HMMM...

LOOK, SAM. MUM'S DONE IT! SHE'S ON HER WAY BACK DOWN NOW.

THE SWORD.

DOES SHE HAVE THE SWORD?

LOOK OUT --

-- SHE'S BEING ATTACKED BY SPARROWS!

DO NOT AIM TO KILL ANY OF THE BIRDS.
SHOOT TO FRIGHTEN THEM OFF!
READY --

"-- FIRE!"

SHE'LL MAKE IT DOWN.
ONE MORE GOOD VOLLEY SHOULD SCARE THEM OFF.
FIRE!

AWK!

AWWWK!

PLOP
AWK -- KILLEE!

I KILLEE YOU!
LET WARBEAK FREE, YOU DIRTY WORM!
PHEW!
WHAT A WILD BUNCH OF SAVAGES THOSE SPARROWS ARE!
JESS!
WHUMP

WHERE IS THE SWORD?
IT WASN'T THERE, MATTHIAS.

I CLIMBED OUT ALONG THE NORTH POINTER AND ACTUALLY SAW THE SHAPE OF THE SWORD IN THE HOLDER, WHERE IT WAS SUPPOSED TO REST. BUT THERE WAS DEFINITELY NO SWORD.
I'M SORRY, MATTHIAS. I TRIED MY BEST.

OF COURSE YOU DID, JESS.
THANK YOU VERY MUCH FOR YOUR VALIANT EFFORTS.
KILLEE MOUSE!
WARBEAK KILLEET!

"IF YOU NEED THIS SPECIAL HERB, SELA --
" -- WHY DON'T YOU SEND YOUR SON, CHICKENHOUND, TO GET IT?"

"NO, I'M AFRAID THAT'S USELESS, SIR. HE'S TOO YOUNG AND INEXPERIENCED.
"I'LL HAVE TO GO MYSELF."
HEH!
STUPID RATS...

ACK!

BE STILL, FOX --
GUKK
-- OR I'LL SNAP YOUR NECK LIKE A DEAD TWIG!

SNIK

YOUR -- UKK
YOUR ABBOT WAS SUPPOSED TO MEET ME WITH A REWARD --

AHA!
CLUNY'S INVASION PLANS!

HERE'S YOUR REWARD, TRAITOR!
WHUMP
TELL THE RATS! TELL THEM --
I REMEMBER THEIR DEFEAT AT THE WALL!

I WISH THAT I WERE YOUNG AND AGILE ONCE AGAIN, SO THAT I COULD ACCOMPANY YOU.

GOOD FORTUNE GO WITH YOU, MATTHIAS.

THANK YOU, METHUSELAH.

COME ON, YOU!

REMEMBER, MATTHIAS -- THE SPARROWS CONSIDER THE ROOF TO BE THEIR TERRITORY.

THE *"SPARRA"* LANGUAGE IS VERY DIFFICULT TO COMPREHEND. WARBEAK, HERE, SHOULD BE ABLE TO HELP YOU --

-- BUT IF SHE CAUSES YOU ANY TROUBLE, DON'T HESITATE TO KICK HER OFF INTO THIN AIR!

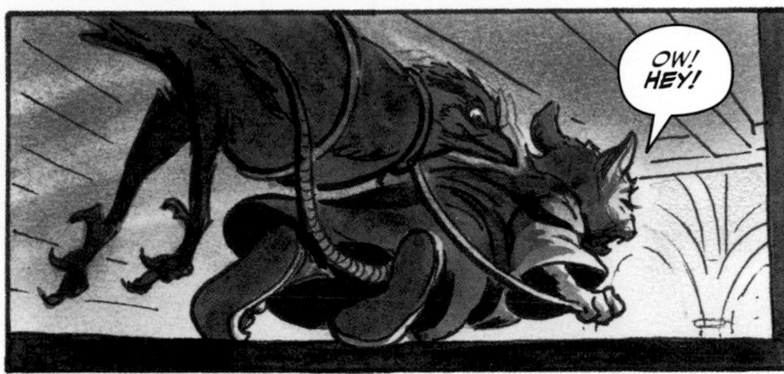
OW! HEY!

KILLEE! AWK!

EEEEEE!

LISTEN, WARBEAK. ONE MORE MOVE LIKE THAT AND IT WILL BE YOUR LAST.
DO YOU HEAR ME?

WARBEAK NOT WANTA DIE. MOUSE WIN!
PULL SPARRA UP. BE GOOD.
GIVE WORD!

HOW GOOD IS THE WORD OF A SPARROW?
SPARRA WORD ALWAYS GOOD.
ME SWEAR BY MOTHER'S EGG. THAT BIG SWEAR!

HA! MATTHIAS ALL RED MOUSE!
YOU SHOULD TALK, WARBEAK -- YOU'RE BLUE ALL OVER. IT'S THESE STAINED GLASS WINDOWS.
UP AHEAD... THERE'S A LOFT DOOR IN THE WALL...

OH, DEAR...

A FOOL, THAT'S WHAT I AM. CLIMBING ALL THIS WAY TO BE BEATEN BY AN OLD LOFT DOOR!
WHY NOT MATTHIAS CUT WARBEAK FREE? THEN FLY WITH SPARRA WINGS AND OPEN LITTLE WORM DOOR.
GIVE WORD!

...
ALL RIGHT.

LONG TIME NO FLY.
ME GOOD, YOU SEE!

WATCH OUT.
DOOR OPEN, FALL ON MOUSE!

WHUMP

WARBEAK -- I CAN NO LONGER KEEP YOU COLLARED.
YOU ARE A FREE SPARROW AND A VERY GOOD FRIEND.
MATTHIAS, MY MOUSE FRIEND.
I NO LEAVE. STAY WITH YOU!

ME KING BULL SPARRA!

MOUSE WORM -- YOU MY PRISONER!

THIS COURT OF SPARRA!

...SO YOU KNOW ABOUT TUNNELING?
AH, THE TUNNELS, YER HONOR. YOU'RE TALKIN' TO THE VERY CREATURE.
FERRETS LIKE ME, STOATS AND WEASELS -- WHY, SURE, WE'RE AS GOOD AS ANY MOLE WHEN IT COMES TO THE TUNNELIN' --
KRASH

WHAT'S GOING ON HERE?
IT'S THESE TWO FOXES, CHIEF. I CAUGHT THEM WITH THEIR EARS AGAINST THE DOOR.
THEY WERE LISTENING IN.

NOT US, SIR. WE WEREN'T EAVESDROPPING.
WE JUST WANTED TO HELP. GIVE US A CHANCE AND WE'LL TUNNEL WITH THE BEST OF THEM!

WHO SAID ANYTHING ABOUT TUNNELING, FOX?
UHHH!

YOU SLIPPED UP, VIXEN, WHEN YOU COPIED MY PLANS FOR AN ATTACK WITH A BATTERING RAM.
NOW YOU KNOW MY *REAL* PLAN: TO TUNNEL INTO REDWALL.

YOU KNOW TOO MUCH. YOU AND YOUR SON PLAYED A DANGEROUS GAME...AND LOST.
NOBODY OUTSMARTS CLUNY.

TAKE THESE MISERABLE TURNCOATS OUT OF MY SIGHT.
YOU KNOW WHAT TO DO.

NO!
NOW...
PLEASE!

...ABOUT THIS *TUNNEL.*

UH -- O KING BULL SPARRA --
I COME TO RETURN ONE OF YOUR BRAVE YOUNG WARRIORS!

YOU LIE, MOUSEWORM -- NOT HELP SPARRA. MOUSE ENEMY!
KING BULL SPARRA SAY KILLEE ENEMY. K-KILLEET!
NO!

NO KILLEE! MOUSE GOOD. SAVE MY EGG SPARRA!
NOT KILLEE MATTHIAS MOUSE! HIM SAVE WARBEAK --

-- GIVE SPARRA WORD TO MOUSE THAT YOU NO KILLEE!

MOUSEWORM --
COME HERE.

KING BULL SPARRA SPARE MOUSE. HOW YOU LIKE HIM FOR PET, MY NIECE?
MOUSE, YOU OBEY MY SISTER AND HER EGGCHICK. FUNNY, HA?
HAHAHA
HAHAHAHA
HA HAHAHA
HAHAHAHAHA
MATTHIAS --

-- YOU SEE WARBEAK AND MOTHER NOT MAKE LAUGH.

DON'T WORRY, MY FRIEND.
AT LEAST I'M ALIVE!

LATER...
COLLAR HURTS... I MEAN, HURT MOUSENECK.
KING SAY YOU WEARA. NO CAN TAKE OFF.
SORRY.

WARBEAK GO HUNTING. BACK SOON!
MATTHIAS SAVE MY WARBEAK. WE HAVE NO SPARRA WARRIOR TO LOOK AFTER US.
WARBEAK BRAVE LIKE FATHER WAS. NOW FATHER, HE DEAD.

DUNWING, LISTEN. I WANT TO TELL YOU A STORY.
ABOUT THE MICE WHO LIVE IN THE ABBEY BENEATH US... AND OF ONE MOUSE IN PARTICULAR CALLED MARTIN THE WARRIOR.

AND ONCE THE TALE HAD BEEN TOLD...
MATTHIAS -- DUNWING KNEW! FIRST YOU COME HERE I SEE BELT YOU WEAR.
IT ALL SAME AS THING BEHIND CHAIR IN KING'S ROOM!
THING BEHIND...

THEN THE SWORD IS HERE?
NO.
YOUNG MOUSE SIT STILL. NOW ME TELL YOU STORY.

MANY TIME AGO, BEFORE MY MOTHER WAS EGG, KING NAMED BLOODFEATHER. HE STEAL SWORD FROM NORTHPOINT.
SWORD HANG IN COURT OF SPARRA. MAKE SPARRA FOLK PROUD, BRAVE FIGHTERS.
BULL SPARRA BECOME KING. HE MUCH SHOWOFF -- WEAR WARRIOR SWORD, LEAVE HEAVY CASE BEHIND IN ROOM.
MY HUSBAND, GREYTAIL, GO LONGA WITH HIM. DIG WORM WITH SWORD.
ONE DAY THEY HUNT IN MOSSFLOWER TREES. GIANTWORM COME, ONE WITH POISONTEETH -- CURL ROUND SWORDHANDLE.
ALLA TIME SAY, "*ASMODEUSSSSS.*"

BULL SPARRA, HE ORDER GREYTAIL GET SWORD BACK. GREYTAIL TRY, BUT WORM BITE WITH POISONTEETH.
MY HUSBAND DIE.

GREYTAIL BE MIGHTY WARRIOR TO FACE POISONTEETH ALONE. YOU GLAD WARBEAK BE HIS EGGCHICK.
MATTHIAS BE GOOD MOUSE.
FATHER DIE SAVING KING BULL SPARRA LIFE. KING MY BROTHER -- HE VOW TAKE CARE OF US.
BUT KING FORGETEE VOWS SOMETIME.

A GIANT WORM WITH POISONOUS TEETH. THAT DESCRIPTION FITS ONLY ONE THING: A SNAKE!
BUT HOW COULD A MERE MOUSE TAKE THE SWORD FROM A THING LIKE THAT?

ELSEWHERE...
UNNHHH...

UUUHHH!
MOTHER...

...YOU OLD FOOL.
YOU'D NEVER HAVE BEEN IN THIS MESS IF YOU'D LET A YOUNGER AND SMARTER FOX HANDLE THINGS!

MAYBE A SILLY BUNCH OF -- UH -- RATS COULD PUT ONE OVER ON SELA.
BUT I'LL SHOW THEM. REVENGE WILL BE MINE!

FIRST, THOUGH...
THE ABBEY...

AND SOON...
WELL, FOX -- WHAT DO YOU WANT FROM US?
NO DOUBT CLUNY YOUR MASTER HAS SENT YOU HERE TO SPY.

CLUNY'S HORDE DID THIS TO ME. MY MOTHER, SELA... THEY KILLED HER.
I KNOW OF CLUNY'S NEW PLANS. CARE FOR ME AND I WILL TELL YOU ALL!

AS YET I DO NOT KNOW THE FULL EXTENT OF YOUR INJURIES. WHEN YOU HAVE RESTED, MY FRIENDS WILL CLEANSE YOU AND DRESS YOUR WOUNDS.
YOU MEAN I CAN STAY?
BUT I HAVEN'T TOLD YOU OF THE NEW PLANS YET!

LISTEN TO ME, MY SON. WE WOULD NOT TURN YOU AWAY FROM OUR GATES, UNLESS YOU WERE AN ENEMY THAT MEANT US HARM.
ALL CREATURES ARE CARED FOR AT REDWALL ABBEY, AND IT IS MY TASK TO CARE FOR THE SICK AND INJURED.

YOU ARE MY RESPONSIBILITY.
WHETHER OR NOT YOU CHOOSE TO GIVE INFORMATION IS A MATTER THAT YOUR OWN HEART MUST DEAL WITH.

THE BATTERING RAM IS ONLY A DECOY.
CLUNY MEANS TO TUNNEL UNDERNEATH YOUR ABBEY WALLS.
I DON'T KNOW WHERE HE PLANS TO START DIGGING, BUT I KNOW THAT HE WILL COME AT YOU FROM UNDER THE GROUND!

CLUNY IS SURELY THE SPAWN OF DARKNESS, MY SON. HE WILL STOP AT NOTHING.
BUT WHY DID YOU CRAWL ALL THE WAY TO REDWALL WITH THIS INFORMATION -- ALMOST AT THE COST OF YOUR LIFE?

BECAUSE THEY KILLED OLD SELA, SIR. SHE WAS MY MOTHER.
I WILL NOT REST UNTIL JUSTICE IS DONE TO HER MURDERERS.

THANK YOU FOR ENTRUSTING YOUR CONFIDENCE IN US, YOUNG ONE.
TRY TO GET SOME REST.
BASIL...
MAY I SPEAK WITH YOU A MOMENT?

HEE HEE HEE HEE HEE!
THERE'S NO FOOL LIKE AN OLD FOOL!

-- STRIKING AN ENLISTED CREATURE!

BAD FORM, OLD CHAP! THUMPING BAD FORM!

GET HIM! GET THAT SPY!

I WANT HIS ***HEAD!***

TCH

WHAT'S THE MATTER?

ISN'T YOUR OWN HEAD GOOD ENOUGH?

NO, I GUESS NOT.
UGLY-LOOKING BRUTE, AREN'T YOU?

WHERE --

WHAT HO, OLD RAT! SHOWING A BIT OF INITIATIVE?

NEVER ASK THE TROOPS TO DO WHAT YOU CAN'T DO YOURSELF AND ALL THAT!
SPLENDID!

NOW, JESS.
NOW!

RRRRRRRIP

SMAKK

RUN FOR IT, JESS.
I'LL HOLD 'EM OFF!

NOT LIKELY, BASIL --

-- IF YOU STAY, THEN SO DO I!

HEAD FOR THE WOODS.
WE'LL MAKE IT TOGETHER!

ARRGHH! KILL HER!
KILL THE DIRTY SQUIRREL!

UH, CHIEF --

" -- SHE'S GONE."

SOON...

GOOD CREATURES.

THE LATE ROSE IS STARTING TO FLOURISH ANEW. EAT TO YOUR HEART'S CONTENT --

I HAVE OUTLIVED SELA, OUTWITTED CLUNY, AND PULLED THE WOOL OVER THE EYES OF AN ABBEYFUL OF MICE.
ONE DAY, THEY WILL SPEAK MY NAME: *CHICKENHOUND,* FOXPRINCE OF THIEVES --
STOP!

STOP, THIEF!
STOP THE FOX!

COME BACK HERE
PUFF
YOU VILLAIN!

YOU YOUNG BLAGGARD!
SO THIS IS HOW YOU REPAY OUR KINDNESS!

YOU ARE FAR WORSE THAN YOUR WICKED MOTHER!

OUT OF MY WAY, YOU DODDERING OLD **FOOL!**

UUUHH!

HEH! DAFT OLD FOOL!
DIDN'T HE REALIZE HE WAS FACING CHICKENHOUND --

-- OVERLORD OF ALL CRIMINALS --

ASMODEUSSSSSSSS!

THE RAFTERS...
MATTHIAS MOUSA SLEEPYHEAD!
GET UP!
* SQUEAK *

TODAY MATTHIAS ESCAPE SPARRA COURT.
ME MAKE PLAN. KING NOT RIGHT TO KEEP MOUSE PRISONER.

A PLAN? WHAT SORT OF PLAN?
ME SEND WARBEAK TO TELL ABBOT TO GETTA BIG RED SQUIRREL. BRING PLENTY CLIMBROPE.
WHEN SHE SEE YOU ON ROOF SHE CLIMB UP, HELP MATTHIAS MOUSE DOWN.

BUT -- WHAT ABOUT THE KING AND HIS WARRIORS?
GREAT FIBBA LIE.
ME WHISPER BIT HERE, THERE, ABOUT GIANT POISONTEETH. SAY HIM LYING HURT DOWN IN MOSSFLOWER TREES, LOOK TO DIE. POISONTEETH HAVE SWORD WITHA, YOU SEE!
SO BULL SPARRA WILL GO CHASING STRAIGHT DOWN INTO THE WOODS WITH HIS WARRIORS. MEANWHILE I WILL ESCAPE OUT ON TO THE ROOF!
MATTHIAS STEAL SWORD CASE FROM KING, QUICKFAST.
THEN CLIMB DOWN OFF ROOF WITH RED SQUIRREL.

DUNWING...
I'M SORRY. HOW DID YOU GUESS THAT I PLANNED TO STEAL THE SCABBARD?
ME KNOW ALLA TIME.

MATTHIAS MOUSE NOT COME TO BRING MY EGGCHICK SAFEHOME. COME FOR SWORD.
NOT GET SWORD -- BUT ALLA SAME, SWORD CASE BELONG TO MICE. YOU MUST TAKE AWAY -- THESE THINGS TROUBLE FOR SPARRA.
HUSBAND DEAD BECAUSE OF SWORD.
MATTHIAS MOUSE!

KING CALL ALLA WARRIOR. WARBEAK GO NOW.
MOUSEFRIEND SET ME FREE. NOW ME SET YOU FREE. ME MEET MATTHIAS MOUSE AGAIN ONE DAY.
MATTHIAS LOOK FOR WARBEAK. SEE SOMEDAY.

BE BRAVE, EGGCHICK. MIGHTY SPARRA WARRIOR.
GREAT FRIEND!
MATTHIAS TAKE CLIMB ROPE. NOT LOSE TIME!

THE SCABBARD OF MARTIN'S SWORD!

IT'S NO GOOD, DUNWING! I'LL NEVER BE ABLE TO DO IT!

CLIMB UP TO GUTTER.

DUNWING HAVE ROPE PLENTY TIGHT HOLD!

JESS!

JESS, UP HERE!

LOOK! I'VE GOT THE SCABBARD!
MOUSEWORM!
KILLEE!

AAAHH!

AAH!
AAHH!

SNAP
OH NO!

MATTHIAS, MATTHIAS...

LATE ROSE! PLEASE TELL ME...
WHERE WILL I FIND THE SWORD?

METHUSELAH!
MATTHIAS, MY FRIEND...I CAN HELP YOU NO MORE. SEEK OUT THE AID OF MARTIN.
I MUST GO NOW.

MARTIN? WHY DO YOU STOP ME FROM GETTING THE SWORD?
MATTHIAS... I AM THAT IS. STAY.
BEWARE OF ASMODEUS!

LET ME GO, MARTIN!
I FEAR NO CREATURE THAT LIVES!
HOLD HIM STILL NOW!

UUH!
WELL, MY SON, YOU ARE BACK WITH US AT LAST.
THAT MUST HAVE HURT --

-- THERE WAS HALF OF A SPARROW'S BEAK LODGED IN YOUR SHOULDER!

YOU HAVE MISSED A LOT, MATTHIAS.
JESS SQUIRREL AND BASIL STAG HARE RECAPTURED OUR TAPESTRY FROM CLUNY.
IT WAS A VERY DARING DEED.

MARTIN'S TAPESTRY, BACK HERE AT THE ABBEY? HOW MARVELOUS!
I'LL BET OLD METHUSELAH IS OVER THE MOON TO HAVE IT BACK!

PLEASE, WOULD YOU LEAVE US ALONE FOR NOW?
I HAVE SOMETHING TO TELL MATTHIAS.

THE NEXT DAY...
"BASIL...
"WHAT DO YOU KNOW ABOUT A POISONOUS SNAKE CALLED ASMODEUS?"

"ASMODEUS? QUITE FRANKLY, OLD CHAP, I THOUGHT THE BLIGHTER HAD DIED YEARS AGO.
"BUT I HAVE A PRETTY FAIR IDEA WHO WILL KNOW.

"IF YOU STRIKE OUT NORTH-EAST ACROSS MOSSFLOWER WOOD, YOU'LL FIND A DESERTED FARMHOUSE. THE CHAP YOU WANT IS A WHOPPING GREAT OWL NAMED CAPTAIN SNOW.
"SHOW HIM THIS MEDAL, DONCHA KNOW. CAPTAIN SNOW GAVE IT TO ME FOR SAVING HIS LIFE."

"MAKE SURE HE SEES THE MEDAL BEFORE HE SEES *YOU* --
" -- OTHERWISE HE'LL EAT YOU ON SIGHT."
AAH!
WHO ARE YOU?

WHY ARE YOU TRESPASSING ON SHREW LAND?

NEVER MIND WHO I AM! WHO DO YOU THINK YOU ARE, YOU LITTLE CREATURE?
I AM GUOSIM.
GUOSIM? WHAT SORT OF A NAME IS THAT?

DON'T YOU KNOW ANYTHING? GUOSIM STANDS FOR *GUERRILLA UNION OF SHREWS IN MOSSFLOWER.*
I COULDN'T CARE LESS WHAT IT STANDS FOR.
MAKE WAY FOR A REDWALL ABBEY WARRIOR. I'M COMING THROUGH!

HANG HIM BY THE TAIL!
BREAK HIS PAWS!
STUFF HIS WHISKERS DOWN HIS EARS!
SKIN HIM ALIVE!
LET ME EXPLAIN -- !

RIGHT, COMRADES. NOW THAT WE KNOW A BIT MORE ABOUT THINGS, LET'S HAVE A SHOW OF PAWS.
ALL THOSE IN FAVOR OF LETTING THE MOUSE GO FREE?
MATTHIAS OF REDWALL, YOU ARE ON OUR LAND. WE WILL ESCORT YOU.
YOU MAY NOT ALWAYS SEE US -- BUT WE WILL BE CLOSE BY.

WHOOPS!

* SQUEAK! *

THE ABBEY.

ON TO REDWALL!

SMASH THE GATES!

KILL, KILL!

CLUNY CLUNY

ATTENTION, MICE!

SURRENDER TO CLUNY THE SCOURGE!

KILL KILL

GO AND BOIL YOUR HEAD, RAT!

" -- WHERE'S THAT BATTERING RAM?"

COME ON, MATES!

LET'S KNOCK ON THE ABBEY DOOR!

END BOOK TWO

BOOK THREE THE WARRIOR
MATTHIAS LAY WET AND STICKY, QUIVERING ALL OVER, DUST AND STRAW CLINGING TO HIS FUR.
PHUT
HE HAD NO CHANCE TO MAKE A RUN FOR IT, AND HE COULD NOT STOP HIS BODY FROM QUAKING BADLY.
HE LAY STARING INTO THE FELINE EYES... GREAT TWIN POOLS OF TURQUOISE FLECKED WITH GOLD...
AND THEN...
UGH! I SIMPLY CANNOT ABIDE THE TASTE OF MOUSE.
FILTHY LITTLE VERMIN. ONE CAN NEVER TELL WHERE THEY'VE BEEN!
WELL, MOUSE? HAVE YOU NOTHING TO SAY FOR YOURSELF?
DON'T YOU THINK YOU SHOULD APOLOGIZE FOR LEAPING INTO MY MOUTH LIKE THAT?

I...I BEG YOUR PARDON, SIR. I SINCERELY HOPE I HAVE NOT DISTURBED YOU.
I AM MATTHIAS OF REDWALL.
I ACCEPT YOUR APOLOGY, MATTHIAS OF REDWALL.
I AM *SQUIRE JULIAN GINGIVERE.*

I HAVE COME SEEKING AN OWL CALLED CAPTAIN SNOW.
CAPTAIN SNOW, EH? THAT OLD MANIAC!
I'VE FORBIDDEN HIM THE USE OF MY BARN.
WHAT A THOROUGHLY DREADFUL BIRD -- HE EATS ANYTHING THAT MOVES OR CRAWLS.

IT IS SO LONELY TRYING TO PRESERVE ONE'S STANDARDS IN A DECAYING WORLD...
COULD YOU TELL ME WHERE I MIGHT FIND HIM, PLEASE?
CAPTAIN SNOW, I MEAN?

SNOW LIVES IN A HOLLOW TREE THESE DAYS.
I'LL STRETCH A POINT AND TAKE YOU THERE - BUT PLEASE DON'T EXPECT ME TO INTRODUCE YOU OR EVEN TALK TO HIM.
WHEN I BARRED SNOW FROM HERE, WE HAD A DREADFUL QUARREL.

SOON...
YOUR FRIENDS THE SHREWS ARE OUT IN FORCE TODAY.
THEY THINK I CAN'T SEE THEM... BUT I DO.

YOU PROBABLY CAN'T SEE CAPTAIN SNOW, BUT HE'S WATCHING US.
BE EXTRA CAREFUL, MATTHIAS. THE OLD GLUTTON WILL MORE THAN LIKELY EAT YOU ON SIGHT.

IF YOU GET THE CHANCE, TELL HIM SQUIRE GINGIVERE SAID THAT HE MUST SURELY ADMIT HE WAS IN THE WRONG AND APOLOGIZE. ONLY THEN CAN WE RESUME OUR FRIENDSHIP AND LIVE TOGETHER IN THE BARN.
GOOD-BYE, MATTHIAS, AND DO TAKE CARE.
GOOD-BYE, JULIAN. AND THANK YOU!

HELLO?
CAPTAIN SNOW?

AAAHHHH!

TRUCE! BASIL STAG HARE SENT ME!
I CLAIM A *TRUCE!*
WHAT DID THE CAT SAY TO YOU, MOUSE?
I WON'T APOLOGIZE TO HIM. I REFUSE TO!

I DON'T CARE IF HE'S GOT MAGIC EYES, POISON TEETH, COILS OF STEEL, OR WHATEVER. I MEAN TO HAVE THAT SWORD!
I'LL FIGHT ASMODEUS AND WIN, TOO!

BET YOU THIS MEDAL THAT I WILL!
DONE!

HOLD ON, OWL. THAT MEDAL IS NOT YOURS TO BET.
IF I SHOULD WIN GAINST ASMODEUS, OU MUST PROMISE N YOUR OATH THAT OU WILL NEVER EAT NOTHER MOUSE OR SHREW OF ANY TYPE.

AGREED. IN FACT --
HA HA HA!
IN FACT, I PROMISE YOU THAT IF YOU DEFEAT THE SNAKE, I'LL ADMIT I WAS WRONG TO THAT STUFFY OLD CAT!

NOW...
TELL ME WHERE I MAY FIND ASMODEUS, CAP'N.

BACK AT THE ABBEY...
REDWALL TO ME! COME ON, MICE!
LET'S GIVE BETTER THAN WE GET!
FIRST RANK, FIRE! DROP BACK, KNEEL AND RELOAD!
SECOND RANK, FIRE!

AAAHHH!

CHIEF, THEY'VE POURED SOME STUFF OVER THE BATTERING RAM. WE CAN'T HOLD ON TO IT -- IT'S LIKE TRYING TO PICK UP A WET EEL.
AND THEN THEY DROPPED A BUCKET OF ***HORNETS ON US. IT'S NOT FAIR!***

THE BATTERING RAM WAS ONLY A DIVERSION, FOOL.
THE REAL THREAT IS WITH KILLCONEY --

" -- AND HIS TUNNELS."
...WHEN YOU BREAK THROUGH INTO THE GROUNDS, MAKE STRAIGHT FOR THE ABBEY BUILDING.
DARKCLAW, TAKE SOME WARRIORS AND FIGHT YOUR WAY THROUGH TO THE GATE. ONCE IT'S OPEN, THE OTHERS WILL BE ABLE TO GET IN.

DIG! DIG!
THOSE STUPID MICE WON'T KNOW WHAT HIT 'EM!

POP
UP WE --

-- GO!?

NO!

A HHH!
AAA HHH!
AAGGHH!

HEY, WHAT'S HAPPENED? COME BACK HERE THIS MINUTE!
WHERE D'YOU THINK YOU'RE ALL GOING?
AAAHHH!

WE DON'T WANT TO DISTURB THE CHIEF ABOUT THIS, DO WE?
I'M ONLY A FERRET -- BUT HE MIGHT NOT THANK US.
AYE, THAT'S TRUE. LET'S LEAVE IT TILL LATER!

THE FOREST...
AHEM -- ER, MATTHIAS...

DID YOU FIND OUT WHERE POISONTEETH IS?
YES.
IN A CAVE IN THE OLD SANDSTONE QUARRY, ACROSS THE RIVER.

CAPTAIN SNOW HAS GIVEN ME HIS PROMISE ON OATH: IF I DEFEAT ASMODEUS, HE WILL NEVER AGAIN TAKE THE LIFE OF A SHREW.
IT WOULD BE A DOUBLE BLESSING FOR YOU -- YOU COULD LIVE IN SAFETY FROM BOTH HIM AND THE SNAKE.
WILL YOU LEAD ME TO THE QUARRY?

MATTHIAS...WE SHREWS OF THE UNION TRY TO RUN OUR LIVES ALONG DEMOCRATIC LINES. YOU MUST NOT THINK TOO HARSHLY OF US.
THE QUARRY ACROSS THE RIVER IS NOT IN SHREW TERRITORY.

LOOK, LOG-A-LOG. DON'T TALK TO ME ABOUT YOUR SILLY RULES: SUBSECTION THREE, PARAGRAPH FOUR, AND ALL THAT NONSENSE.
YOU ARE EITHER WITH ME OR AGAINST ME.
MATTHIAS -- MY FRIEND --

-- WE HAVE TAKEN A VOTE, AND WE ARE WITH YOU TO A SHREW. TOOTH, CLAW, AND NAIL.
LEAD ON, BOLD WARRIOR!

WELL, LET'S GET STARTED.
WE'VE GOT AN ADDER TO FIGHT AND A SWORD TO WIN!

LATER...
LOG-A-LOG!
IT WAS HIM! GIANT POISONTEETH, THE SNAKE!
GUOSIM!

I DIDN'T SPOT HIM UNTIL IT WAS TOO LATE. HE'S TAKEN MINGO -- GAVE HIM THE MAGIC EYES, THEN BIT HIM AND DRAGGED HIM OFF!

RIGHT HERE!
YOU CAN SEE THE GREAT SLITHERING MARKS!

LOOK!

SUPPOSING POISONTEETH DECIDES TO HUNT SOME MORE?
I HAVE A FEELING HE WON'T, GUOSIM. HE'S GOTTEN A FULL DAY'S HUNT IN.

AAAAAHHHH!
GUOSIM!

LOG-A-LOG... I THINK WE'VE FOUND THE ENTRANCE...
...TO THE LAIR OF ASMODEUS POISONTEETH!

SOON...

NO SIGN OF GUOSIM YET.

YOU TAKE THE LEFT AND I'LL TAKE THE RIGHT.

ASMODEUSSSSSSSSSSSSS!

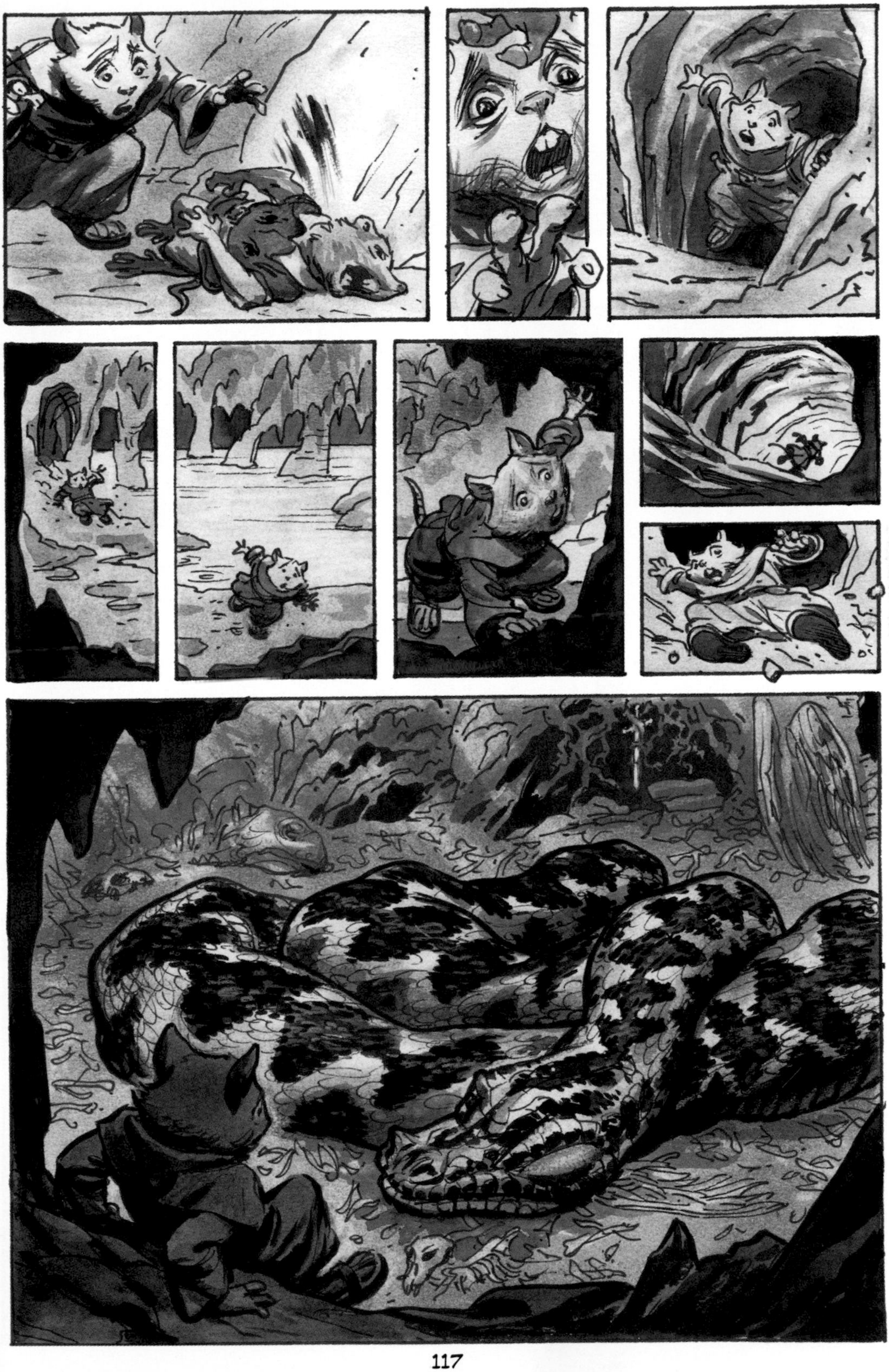

HE'S ASLEEP.
AND OVER THERE... ON THE WALL...

THE SWORD!

ASMODEUSSCCCCSS!

ASMODEUSSSSSSSSSS!

COME ON!

LET'S GET OUT OF THIS PLACE!

STAY OUT OF THE WAY, SHREW. THERE'S NO MORE RETREATING.

ALL ENDS HERE!

LOOK AT ME, MY LITTLE FRIEND. I CAN SEE THAT YOU ARE A GREAT WARRIOR.

YOU ARE NOT AFRAID TO GAZE INTO MY EYES.

I AM THAT IS!

WHY DO YOU SLEEP? THERE IS A WARRIOR'S WORK TO BE DONE HERE!

MARTIN!

PICK UP YOUR SWORD, MATTHIAS!

"STRIKE!"

"STRIKE FOR REDWALL!
"STRIKE AGAINST EVIL!
"STRIKE FOR THE SHREWS!
"STRIKE FOR DEAD GUOSIM!
"STRIKE AS METHUSELAH WOULD HAVE WANTED!
"STRIKE AGAINST CLUNY THE SCOURGE AND TYRANNY!
"STRIKE --
" -- UNTIL THE SWORD FALLS FROM YOUR PAWS!
"STRIKE FOR THE WORLD OF LIGHT AND FREEDOM!"

OUTSIDE THE ABBEY WALLS...
YOU -- DORMOUSE --
-- WHAT'S YOUR NAME?

P-P-PLUMPEN, SIR.

AND WHAT ARE THESE OTHER MISERABLE CREATURES TO YOU, PLUMPEN?
MY FAMILY, SIR.
OH, PLEASE, SIR, SPARE THEM. I BEG YOU!

TELL ME, PLUMPEN...

...WHAT WOULD YOU DO TO SAVE THEM?

REDWALL'S RAMPARTS.
FRIENDS --
IT WILL AVAIL CLUNY LITTLE TO PUT THE ABBEY UNDER A STATE OF SIEGE. AS YOU KNOW, REDWALL IS VIRTUALLY SELF-SUPPORTING.

HOWEVER, THE WALLS MUST ALWAYS BE GUARDED. I LEAVE IT TO YOU, MY CAPTAINS.
STAY EVER VIGILANT AGAINST CLUNY AND HIS HORDE -- AND I KNOW THAT WE WILL SOON SEE THE DAY WHEN THE ENEMY ARE FORCED TO GO ELSEWHERE, AND LEAVE REDWALL IN PEACE.

YAY!
NEVER.
CLUNY WON'T LEAVE US ALONE UNTIL EITHER WE ARE DEAD --

-- OR HE IS.

THAT NIGHT...

SQUEEKA
SQUEEKA

SQUEEEEK

SIR? I...I'VE CARRIED OUT MY PART...
SURELY NOW YOU WILL SPARE MY FAMILY?

BASH

AT LAST!
REDWALL IS MINE!

WHAT --

YOU --

LET ME -- OW!
LET ME OUT OF HERE! I'LL -- AHH! I'LL KILL YOU ALL!

WELL, WARRIOR MOUSE. WHAT DO YOU THINK OF YOUR BRAVE REDWALL DEFENDERS NOW?
NOT MUCH, I IMAGINE!

HENCEFORTH THIS PLACE SHALL BE KNOWN AS HALL OF THE SCOURGE!
NO MORE WILL THE ABBEY BE KNOWN AS REDWALL -- IT SHALL BE CALLED CLUNY'S CASTLE!

NO MORE WILL YOU HAUNT MY DREAMS!
A VOICE INSIDE ME SAID THAT BEFORE SUNSET THIS DAY, I WOULD BE FREE OF MY NIGHTMARES FOREVER!
WHAT DO YOU THINK OF THAT?!

OH, MIGHTY WARRIOR --
-- SAVIOR OF THE SHREWS, SLAYER OF POISONTEETH; HE WHO SPEAKS WITH CATS --
-- FRIENDMAKER OF OWLS AND UNITER OF --
OH, SHUT UP, YOU NOISY LITTLE DEVIL!
AT LEAST JULIAN AND CAP'N SNOW SEEM TO HAVE RESOLVED THEIR DIFFERENCES.

WARBEAK SPARRA! THATTA YOU, OLD WORM WARRIOR!
MATTHIAS MOUSE! OLD WORMFRIEND!
BIG FAT WARRIOR NOW!

WARBEAK QUEEN NOW -- KING BULL SPARRA DIE. SPARRAS LIKE NEW QUEEN.
BUT REDWALL HAVE BIG TROUBLE.

MICE BRAVE WARRIORS, BUT RATWORM MAKE LOTTA PLANS. CATCH ABBEY -- BE INSIDE REDWALL.
MATTHIAS MOUSE COME QUICK. BRING SWORD!

WHAT'S SHE SAYING, MATTHIAS?
IT'S MY HOME. REDWALL.
CLUNY THE SCOURGE HAS CAPTURED IT!
I BRING ALLA TRIBE SPARRA WARRIOR. WE COME, HELP.
SHREWMOUSE HELP YOU?

WE'RE OFF TO THE ABBEY AT REDWALL! I WANT NO ARGUMENT OR VOTES!
TELL EVERY SHREW TO BE FULLY ARMED. WE MUST SAVE MATTHIAS'S FRIENDS!

DEFENDERS OF REDWALL --
HEAR ME!

I HAVE COME TO SETTLE WITH YOU!
LEAVE GOOD FATHER ABBOT AND FACE *ME,* COWARD.

MATTHIAS!

WHO *ARE* YOU?
YOU -- YOU'RE SOMETHING OUT OF MY DREAMS --

I AM THAT IS.
MARTIN, MATTHIAS -- CALL ME WHAT YOU WILL, RAT. IT WAS WRITTEN, LONG AGO, THAT YOU AND I WOULD MEET.

NO! I AM NOT ASLEEP!
SEIZE HIM!

HALT! I WILL SLAY ANY INVADER THAT MOVES.
THIS IS BETWEEN YOU AND ME, CLUNY. YOUR ARMY WILL NOT INTERFERE.

BONG
BONG
BONG

REDWALL.

"REDWALL."

REDWALL!
STRIKE FOR REDWALL!

I MAY LOSE SKIRMISHES, MOUSE --
-- BUT I ALWAYS WIN THE WAR!

URGGHHKK*

WHAT -- ?

AAARRHHH!
WHUMP

BONG
BONG

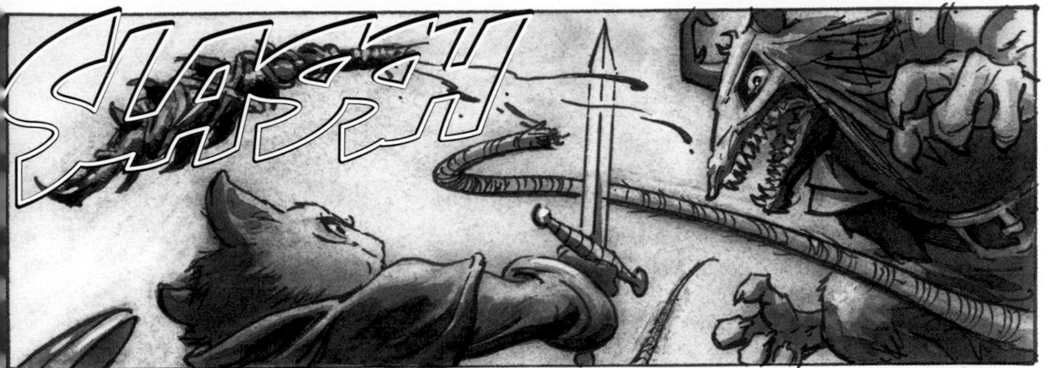
SLASSSH

BONG
BONG

AAH!
OH!

BONG
BONG
BONG

WHAT --

NGGHHH!

UHH!

THERE'S NO WAY OUT UP THERE, MOUSE!
YOU'RE AS GOOD AS DEAD NOW!

LOOK, MOUSE! I'VE GOT YOUR LITTLE FAT FRIEND!
THROW THE SWORD DOWN OR I'LL SPIKE HIM LIKE A LOLLIPOP!

ALL RIGHT, RAT! YOU WIN!
LET THE FRIAR GO, AND I PROMISE ON MY HONOR AS A WARRIOR THAT I'LL COME DOWN!

THE HONOR OF A WARRIOR.
GET OUT OF MY SIGHT, YOU LITTLE WRETCH!

SNISSHHH
COME ON DOWN, MOUSE!
CLUNY THE SCOURGE IS WAITING FOR YOU!

BONG

I KEPT MY PROMISE TO YOU, CLUNY.
I CAME DOWN.
MATTHIAS... MY SON...

...I SEE YOU HAVE RESTORED THE SWORD OF MARTIN TO OUR ABBEY.
IS YOUR MISSION COMPLETED THEN?
YES, FATHER.

CLUNY THE SCOURGE IS DEAD.
I HAVE DONE MY TASK.

SO HAVE I, MY SON.
SO HAVE I...
FATHER ABBOT -- YOU MUST LIVE!

CLUNY MAY BE DEAD...BUT HIS POISON-BARBED TAIL HAS DONE ITS WORK ON ME.
I AM NOT LIKE THE SEASONS, MY OLD FRIEND. I CANNOT GO ON FOREVER.

MATTHIAS, BRAVE ONE... WIPE AWAY YOUR TEARS. DEATH IS ONLY PART OF LIFE.
TELL ME... CAN YOU SEE THE LATE ROSE?
YES, FATHER.
IT IS IN FULL BLOOM NOW.

WHAT A GREAT PITY THAT IT TOOK SO MUCH BLOODSHED TO UNITE US ALL.
HENCEFORTH THE SPARROWS MAY SHARE OUR FOOD AND USE OUR ABBEY. NOT ONLY THE ROOF, BUT ALL OF IT.
THESE GOOD GUERRILLA SHREWS ALSO -- NO LONGER WILL THEY BE AS GYPSIES ROAMING THE WOODS.
THEY WILL HAVE A PROPER HOME HERE AT REDWALL AS LONG AS THEY WISH.

MATTHIAS...THIS ABBEY NEEDS YOU. BUT NOT AS A BROTHER.
I NAME YOU, MATTHIAS, THE WARRIOR MOUSE OF REDWALL, CHAMPION OF OUR ORDER.
FROM THIS DAY YOU WILL DEFEND THIS ABBEY AND ALL OF ITS CREATURES FROM EVIL AND WRONG.
YOUR SWORD SHALL BE KNOWN FAR AND WIDE AS "RATDEATH."

BROTHER ALF...YOU WILL TAKE MY PLACE AS ABBOT.
AND CORNFLOWER... A WARRIOR NEEDS A GOOD WIFE. YOU ARE THE BEAUTY THAT WILL GRACE REDWALL AND RULE THE HEART OF OUR MATTHIAS.

AND YOU, CONSTANCE...MY OLDEST FRIEND... DO ME ONE LAST SERVICE.
LIFT MY HEAD A LITTLE AND I WILL TELL YOU WHAT MY FAILING EYES CAN SEE... BEFORE I LEAVE YOU.

AH YES...I SEE THE MOST BEAUTIFUL SUMMER DAY OF MY LIFE.
THE SUN SHINES WARMLY UPON US. THE FRIENDS I KNOW AND LOVE ARE ALL ABOUT ME.

LIFE IS GOOD, MY FRIENDS. I LEAVE IT TO YOU.
DO NOT BE SAD, FOR MINE IS A PEACEFUL REST. AND REDWALL... OUR HOME...

THE END